in the same series

Sam Pig and his Fiddle
Magic Water
The Christmas Box

The Adventures of Sam Pig

Sam Pig and the Hurdy-Gurdy Man

Alison Uttley

Illustrated by Graham Percy

faber and faber

LONDON · BOSTON

First published in 1942
by Faber and Faber Limited
3 Queen Square London WC1N 3AU
This edition first published in 1988

Printed in Great Britain by
W. S. Cowell Ltd Ipswich

British Library Cataloguing in Publication Data

Uttley, Alison
Sam Pig and the hurdy-gurdy man. –
(The Adventures of Sam Pig).
I. Title   II. Percy, Graham
823'.912[J]   PZ7

ISBN 0–571–15076–4

Sam Pig and the Hurdy-Gurdy Man

The little country road linked village to hamlet, and along it travelled farmers' carts, wagons, horses, and ordinary people going about their daily business. Fields stretched on either side, with hedges of wild roses and bitter-sweet, with ditches of meadowsweet and rushes. The road ran like a white ribbon in the green countryside.

Along this road one summer's day there came a small figure in check trousers and wide sun-hat. By his way of walking anyone could recognize little Sam Pig. Usually Sam took the field paths,

the tracks used by animals, the lonely ways where the only folk one would meet were foxes and hedgehogs and tramps and pedlars and farm men. This day Sam went on the road for a special reason. He walked at a good pace, keeping close to the hedge, singing a song, dancing a few steps now and then, calling to bird and beast in the field.

The hedge came to an end, and a low stone wall began. It was a very old wall, green with stonecrops and ferns, rosy with Robin-run-in-the-hedge, and purple with toadflax. The flowers made a patchwork of colour on the ancient wall. The stones were bound together by a tangled web of roots and flowers which had grown there undisturbed for a hundred years.

Sam Pig sat down on this little wall. It was so low he could rest his feet on the ground. It was as comfortable as an easy chair, with its mossy-cushioned stones.

Sam took a small notebook and a pencil from his pocket.

He was going to write down all the things that passed along the road that morning. He sat there waiting, watching the bend in the road. It was

very quiet, with only the sound of the river murmuring as it fell over the distant rocks, and the hum of the insects in the grasses.

Sam licked the pencil and waited. After a long time a cart came slowly along the road, and Sam wrote down 'cart'. Next came a high-wheeled yellow gig with a prancing horse, well-groomed and beautiful. Sam noted it in his book, in his own special writing. After another long wait came an ancient motor car, and then a donkey-cart. So the country traffic moved along that winding road among wild roses and violets, and

some people nodded to Sam, and cried, 'How' do?' and others never saw him at all. He sat very still, like a part of the lichened mossy wall, intent on his work, and naturally it took a long time to write each word.

Of course Sam didn't write as you and I write, for he had never been to school. He made little pictures, which were just as good as words and twice as nice. There was a square cart for the farmer's cart, and a long cart for the brewer's dray, and a couple of little wheels for a bicycle. The best word was the donkey-cart, but Sam made a rag-bag for a beggar who lurched past and a sun-bonnet for a little girl who dawdled along with many a backward glance at little Sam sitting on the wall.

Well, Sam made the list, and he was thinking of going home to show it to Brock when somebody else came along the road. It was a humped figure who limped very slowly.

'I'll wait for this one and then I'll go,' said Sam, licking his pencil hopefully. He had seen neither wizard nor fairy nor giant. They don't walk the highroads in these days, and Sam was curious about this creature coming. Then Sam saw that the hump was a kind of box the stranger carried, slung on his shoulder by a strap. There was a wooden leg attached to it. Sam was so much excited over this box, with its painted front, that he forgot to write anything in his book.

The man came up to him and stopped. He slipped the strap from his shoulder and took off his old green hat. He looked very tired and dusty.

'A hot day, mate,' he remarked. 'Hot work carrying all this 'ere.'

'Yes, sir,' said Sam.

'Can you guess what this is?' continued the man.

'No, sir,' said Sam.

'It's a hurdy-gurdy. Have you ever seen a hurdy-gurdy, my lad?'

'No, sir,' said Sam, his eyes popping with wonder.

The man sat down on the wall by Sam's side. He wiped his face and neck with his red handkerchief, and Sam saw how thin and weary he was.

'I could do with a drink. I'm parched. How far is it to the next village, mate?' asked the man.

'A few miles,' said Sam. 'I could get you a drink if you've got a cup, sir.'

The man opened a sack and took out an enamel mug. Sam ran off to the field close by where there was a spring of fresh cold water, icy from the depths of the earth. He carried it carefully to the thirsty hurdy-gurdy man.

'Thank you. Thank you, mate. I've not tasted water like this spring water since I was a little nipper like you living in the country,' said the man. Then he hesitated and peered at Sam more closely.

'Well, not like you, for I must say you've got big ears and an uncommonly ugly face.'

'Yes, sir,' said Sam.

The man drained his mug and put it away.

'Now, for that little attention, I'll tell you what I'll do. I'll play you a tune on my hurdy-gurdy. Would you like that?'

'Oh yes, sir,' said Sam, clapping his hands.

So the man put the wooden leg under the hurdy-gurdy and turned the handle. Such a jolly tune came rippling out, in a fountain of little notes, Sam could hardly keep himself from dancing.

But the lovely music went wrong, it stammered, and some notes dropped away, and others ran into one another. The hurdy-gurdy was old, its tunes were cracked, its best days were done. It tried hard, but it couldn't manage. It was a pity, for it was a very nice old hurdy-gurdy.

'Well, I must be going, mate,' said the man, rising slowly to his feet. 'I'm tired and I could sit here all today and all tomorrow. I could sleep here.'

'Why don't you?' asked Sam.

'I've got my living to earn, my bread and cheese and drop of beer.'

He hoisted the box on his shoulder, and took up the sack. He looked so tired Sam was sorry for him.

'Would you like someone to help you?' asked Sam timidly.

'Well, I should, but I can't pay anything. I've taken nothing today, and that water is the first drink that has passed my lips. I must get on to the village and earn my meat.'

'I'll go with you,' said Sam. 'I can help a bit.'

So away with the hurdy-gurdy man went Sam. The little pig wasn't afraid, for the man's face was kind.

Sam carried the sack, which held the mug, a clean shirt, and a pair of Sunday trousers. They talked as they went along – at least the man talked and Sam listened. He told Sam about the places he had seen on the road, little stone Cotswold villages, and beautiful towns, and slow-moving rivers, and deep woods. He had played his hurdy-gurdy in every village and now he was moving north to the hills and high moors and wild rivers.

As he talked they came to the gates of the Big House, and they both stared up the drive.

'Will you play there?' asked Sam hopefully. 'If we can get past the lodge safely, we can play to the cook. She's a friend of mine, an Irishwoman.'

The lodge-keeper wasn't in sight, so they went through the massive gates and up the long drive

to the Big House. Sam led the way to the back door. The hurdy-gurdy man set up his musical box and turned the handle. The gay, crooked, broken little tunes came tumbling out. They were lovely and they were wrong, tantalizing with their confusion. The cook came to the door, and after her came the two little blue-clad kitchen-maids.

'Glory be, I bethought me 'twas the little pigs squealing here, and they after being killt,' said she. 'I'll give ye a penny to go away with that hurdy-gurdy of yours, me man.'

Then she caught sight of little Sam Pig, smiling up at her with his wide mouth and innocent blue eyes.

'Arrah! If it isn't the little Pigwiggin! If it isn't the little cratur as fell into the puddin' bowl and got mistook for a Leprechaun an' all! Indade, and it's welcome you are, and plase to forget the hard words I said about your organ there. Your tunes are in need of a plumber, I'm thinking. It's tarrible quare they are, lepping about like a mad Mooley cow.'

'I thought you would like to hear the music,' said Sam, disappointedly.

'Indade an' I do. But if the misthress hears ever a squeak of it she'll be sending you off double quick. So hould your whist a minute while I'm afther getting you a sup of tay and a bite. Come ye in.'

They followed the kind cook down the stone passage to the big kitchen. They sat down by the fire and she made them tea and gave them food. The hurdy-gurdy man ate ravenously, and the cook looked pityingly at him.

'It's famished ye are. You look tired to the bone,' said she.

'Nay, I've got my living to earn. I can't lay up,' said the man.

She got her purse from the kitchen drawer and gave him a few pence. Then she sent him on his way.

'Good-bye, hurdy-gurdy man. Good-bye, little Pigwiggin, and God be with you,' said she.

They went down the drive, but the lodge-keeper was waiting for them with angry words. They went to the village, but everybody was too busy to give money to a cracked old hurdy-gurdy. Sam held out the mug and rattled a penny in it, but at the end of the day there was only fivepence in it.

'You'd best be going home, young Sam,' said the hurdy-gurdy man. 'Thank you for your company. You've helped me quite a lot.'

'What will you do, Mister Hurdy-gurdy man?'

'Oh, I shall have a bite and then sleep under the hedge and struggle on,' said the man wearily.

'I know a nice place for you. I know a barn with hay in it. Would you like that?' asked Sam.

'I should indeed,' said the man.

'Then I'll wait while you have your supper and I'll take you there. It's at Woodseats Farm, where Farmer Greensleeves lives. He's a friend of mine, like Sally and all of them.'

'Well, that would suit me down to the ground,' said the man.

He went to the inn and had his bread and cheese. Then he walked back with Sam. This time they went by the little paths, on grass that was soft to the man's feet.

Sam saw the farmer, and he ran across to ask permission.

'Of course, Sam Pig, any friend of yours is welcome,' said Farmer Greensleeves, affably. So

Sam took the hurdy-gurdy man to the big barn, and fetched him a mug of milk and a hunch of cake from the farmhouse.

'I shall be all right tomorrow, Sam,' said the man, lying down in the sweet-smelling hay. 'A good night will set me up.'

'There's just one thing,' said Sam. 'Will you lend me the hurdy-gurdy for tonight? I want to play to my brothers. I'll bring it back tomorrow.'

'Yes, take it. It's so cracked you can't make it any worse. Take it, Sam,' said the man, and he fell asleep.

Sam staggered slowly away with the hurdy-gurdy on his back. It took a long time to get home, but he was excited at the thought of the surprise he had in store for Brock and the family.

He walked softly up the path, set up the hurdy-gurdy, and began to play. The door was flung open, and the three little pigs came tumbling out, shrieking with joy.

'Good gracious, Sam! You did startle us! What is this magical box? Oh how lively it is! Let me

try,' they called, and they took turns to wind the handle, and the little cracked tunes came jumbling out higgledy-piggledy to their delight.

'Sam,' said Brock as he listened. 'It sounds a bit cracked to me.'

'Never mind. We love it,' said the pigs.

'I think that hurdy-gurdy has seen its best days. It must be fifty years old,' said Brock, looking at it.

'We love it,' said the pigs again.

All evening they played, but when the sun went down and they came in to supper, Brock took the hurdy-gurdy to pieces. He worked at it for an hour and then he carried it off to the woods.

'I'll put some new tunes in this hurdy-gurdy,' he thought.

He let the wind blow into it, and the nightingale sing into it. He let the brook murmur by it, and the trees rustle there. Then he brought it back to the house.

'Play one more tune before we go to bed,' begged the little pigs.

'All right. Now listen,' said Brock. He turned the handle and the most lovely music came out, far sweeter and clearer than ever before. Nothing cracked or false was left. The Badger had put the music of the woods into the old hurdy-gurdy. There was a nightingale singing in the background, and a blackbird fluting a song. There was sunshine and May Day in it. There was the harp of the trees, and the murmur of wind and water all mingled with the original airs of the little organ.

'What have you done?' asked Sam. 'It's quite different. It's beautiful now.'

'I've mended it,' said Brock. 'If I can mend broken whistles and broken hearts, I can surely mend a broken hurdy-gurdy.'

Sam carried it back to the barn the next morning. The hurdy-gurdy man was asleep, but he awoke when Sam opened the door and let in a flood of sunshine.

'How have you slept?' asked Sam.

'Champion! I feel a different man. I can face anything now,' said the man, stretching himself and standing up to shake the hay from his hair.

'Let's go to the farm and play them a tune,' said Sam. 'It will please them.'

'Maybe they won't be so pleased when they hear my poor old hurdy-gurdy,' laughed the man ruefully.

They walked across to the farmhouse and the man played the hurdy-gurdy.

'What have ye done to it?' he asked, as he turned the handle. 'Nay, this is a fair treat to listen to. It's all changed. It's better than ever it was. There are the old tunes made lovely. What have ye done?' he asked, amazed.

'It was Brock the Badger who did it,' said Sam. 'He mended it for you. He said you would never lack money or friends while you played those tunes, for they will bring back good days to the memory of listeners. He said all the world will want to hear your hurdy-gurdy now.'

It was true. The hurdy-gurdy man never lacked a kind friend and money in his purse. He went through all the villages in England and

Ireland, playing his tunes to the people, and giving joy to the listeners. Every year he came back to the farm, and then Sam Pig and Brock the Badger met him and heard his tales, and turned the handle of the little hurdy-gurdy for their own pleasure. Out came the rippling dancing tunes which made the children dance and the women smile in every cottage of the land.